Listen to the Rain

Listen to the Rain

By Bill Martin Jr. and John Archambault
Illustrated by James Endicott

Henry Holt and Company
New York

Listen to the rain,
the whisper of the rain,

the slow soft sprinkle,
the drip-drop tinkle,

the first wet whisper of the rain.

Listen to the rain,
the singing of the rain,

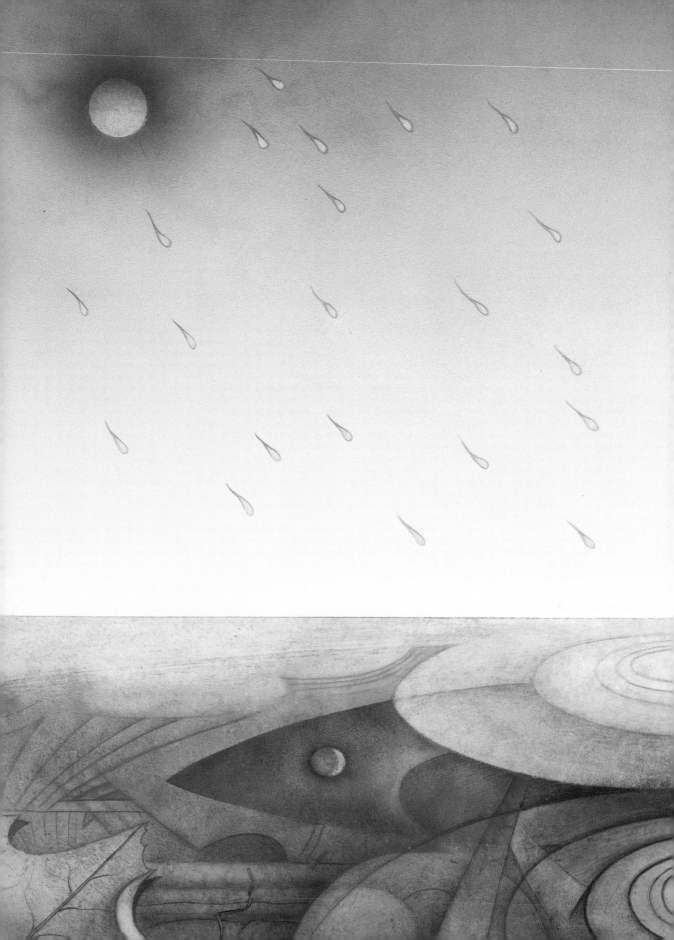

the tiptoe pitter-patter,
the splish and splash and splatter,

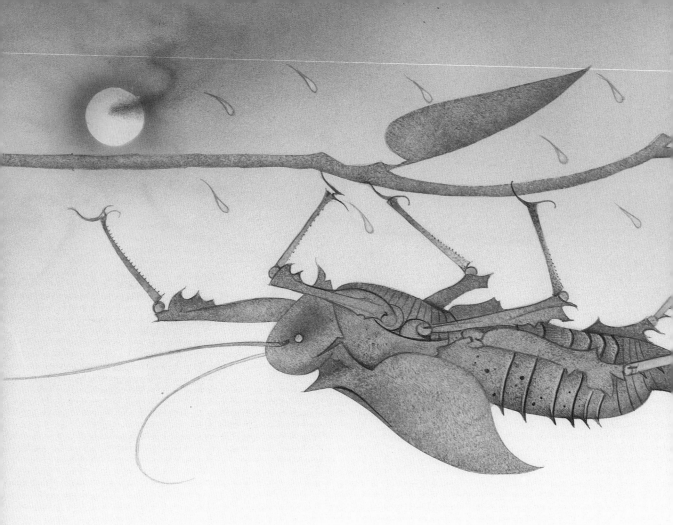

the steady sound,
the singing of the rain.

Listen to the rain,
the roaring pouring rain,

the hurly-burly
topsy-turvy
lashing gnashing teeth of rain,

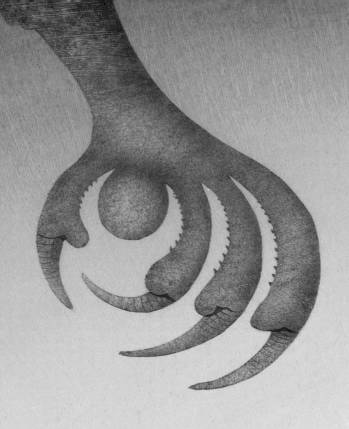

the lightning-flashing
thunder-crashing
sounding pounding roaring rain,

leaving all outdoors a muddle,
a mishy mushy muddy puddle.

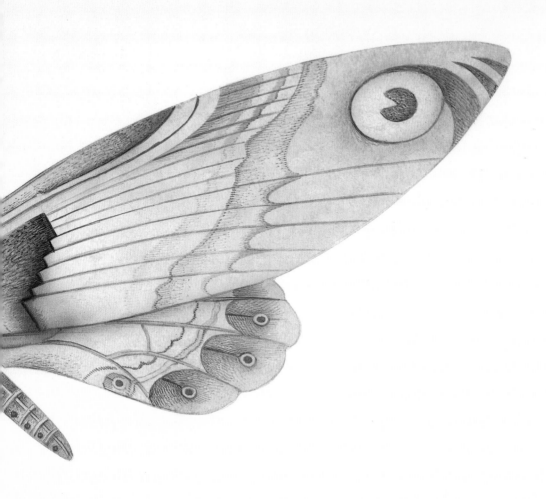

Listen to the quietude,
the silence and the solitude
of after-rain,

the dripping, dripping, dropping,
the slowly, slowly stopping

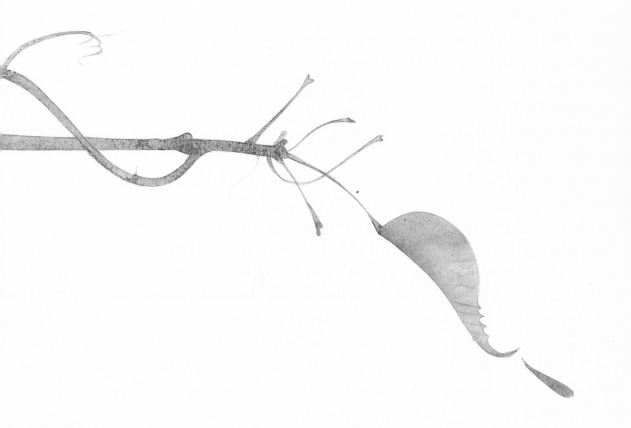

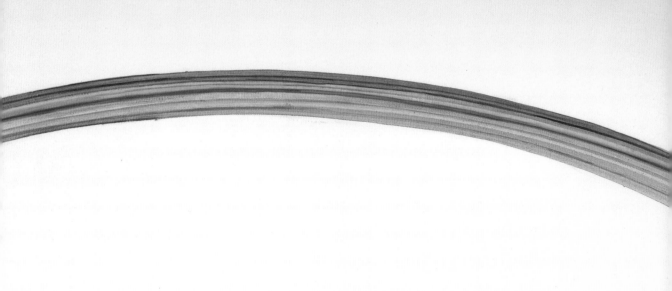

the fresh

    wet

        silent

            after-time

                of rain.

To Andy Bingham
who
on a rainy day
locked us in a room
and said
Write!

—John and Bill

Text copyright © 1988 by Bill Martin Jr. and John Archambault
Illustrations copyright © 1988 by James Endicott
All rights reserved, including the right to reproduce this book
or portions thereof in any form. This book has been published
simultaneously in a different format by DLM Teaching Resources.
Published by Henry Holt and Company, Inc., 115 West 18th Street, New York,
New York 10011. Published in Canada by Fitzhenry & Whiteside Limited,
195 Allstate Parkway, Markham, Ontario L3R 4T8.

Library of Congress Cataloging in Publication Data
Martin, Bill.
Listen to the rain / by Bill Martin Jr. and John Archambault;
illustrated by James Endicott.
Summary: Describes the changing sounds of the rain, the slow soft
sprinkle, the drip-drop tinkle, the sounding pounding roaring rain,
and the fresh wet silent after-time of rain.
[1. Rain and rainfall—Fiction.   2. Sound—Fiction.   3. Stories in
rhyme.]   I. Archambault, John.   II. Endicott, James R., ill.
III. Title.
PZ8.3.M4113Li   1988
[E]—dc19   88-6502

ISBN: 0-8050-0682-6

Printed in the United States of America
15   14   13   12   11   10   9   8   7   6